Prologue
(that's the bit before the story)

You find yourself waiting in line to enter the Savoy Ballroom. Enticing musical notes drift out of the dance hall and into your shoes. The notes *swirl* around your feet like something out of a fairy tale.

The notes **shake** your pinkie toe, then your ... other middle toes until—

Do those middle toes have names?

Sorry, sorry. Back to setting the scene. The notes **shake** and **shimmy** until they reach your big toe—you are full-on grooving in line.

Get ready to groove all the way into the Savoy—a musical adventure awaits!

"Ladies and Gentlemen, I am happy to present the one, the only . . . .

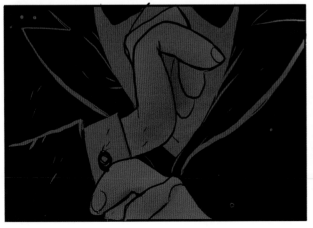

What? "Ladies and Gentlemen, I am happy to present the one, the only" who? We only saw snippets! There were hands and a bow tie and whatever those flap parts of a coat are called.

And what was that stick-looking thing? A wand? A chopstick flying solo for the evening?

Wait. That would be a weird thing for people to get excited about.

Is someone performing a musical about a chopstick looking for its other half?

Well, you'd better find out.

But first you have to read the backstory. To make it even more tedious than it's already going to be, try using your nondominant hand to flip the pages with chopsticks.

Psst, you—yes, you!—pay attention to the orange words.

Challenge accepted?

So, without further ado:

Backstory

This is **Perri Petunia III**—those lines mean "the third." She is twelve years old. She insists on saying twelve and three-quarters. She likes reading. But she only says that to adults, because they like to hear things like that. She prefers going on adventures with her brother, Archer. And playing softball.

This is **Archer.** He is nine. He's crazy about danger and adventure. He likes going on adventures to find his favorite things: pizza, goofy objects, and maps. He hates adventures that lead him to his least favorite things: vegetables, vegetables, and vegetables. He lettuce know that he really hates vegetables.

Yep, more backstory (sigh)

A lifetime ago, when she was seven years old, Eliza Effervescent—Aunt Bubbles to Perri and Archer—found a black silky hat that looked like a chimney pot. It kindled her love of collecting. Her wacky world of wonders began as a modest shack of shocking souvenirs. Then it morphed into a maze of mysteries until, finally, its size challenged the finest hotels in the world. It needed a new name—**"Lost & Found: The Effervescent Emporium of Curiosities."**

⟵ This is Aunt Bubbles, donning her Teasmaid Hat*

*patent pending

10

Even more backstory?! When will it end?!

Short story long: One of the most special, fantastic, un-be-*lieve*-able treasures arrived only two years ago. The story begins as most great stories do: It was a dark and stormy night. A woman hooked and crooked like a question mark entered Lost & Found. She opened a velvet box and bestowed a magical gift on Perri and Archer—a set of books that allowed them to travel through time. She said, "The pages of *The World Book* will *flutter*. The old grandmother clock will

BRONG and BRONG.

Delicate bubbles will ooze from the clock's face. Lost & Found will fade away, and your adventure will begin."

Short story shorter: A bent woman gave two kids a time-traveling device.

Chapter 1: Yowza. That was long. Let's get to the good stuff.

Perri looked her opponent up and down. She knew she could take her.

Inhale.

E x h a l e .

Inhale.

E x h a l e .

Thousands of eyes were on her. And let's not forget the viewers at home. Was Archer watching? Was Aunt Bubbles watching? Was her elementary-school softball coach watching? Middle-school? High-school?!

She peered under the brim of her cap to see Olive, her trusted catcher. Olive quickly flashed four fingers below her mitt. Perri agreed—the tricky shot was their game-winning pitch.

She fired her

curviest,

pitch. The ball challenged the speed of a hummingbird's wings, wove between the tiniest insects, and looped over and under the wind.

SMACK!

The ball hit Olive's glove.

The crowd…went…

WILD!

Perri's teammates lifted her in the air. They cheered

Perr-i!
Perr-i!
Perr-i!

She had finally won the Women's College World Series!

A marching band 500-strong took the field. They were led by TRIUMPHANT baton twirlers. Not only Perri's teammates chanted her name, but the whole stadium.

Perr-i!
Perr-i!
Perr-i!

Acrobats swung from the lights, *leaping* and *looping* through the night sky. Peacocks strutted their stuff and escorted Perri and her teammates to the podium. There, they were greeted by golden meerkats holding golden medals. Balloons and confetti showered Perri and her adoring fans. Streamers, sunflower seeds, and sheer delight mixed together to bring Perri to tears as she ascended the stage to claim her trophy.

Upon being presented with her much-anticipated award, she hoisted it into the air. But the crowd almost immediately quieted.

"Wait, what? What's happening? Why are the chants stopping? Why is the trophy slipping from my hands? Why is the smell of popcorn no longer wafting through the air?! I *am* taking you out to the ballgame! I am! I am!"

Perri shot up.

It was all a dream.

She sighed a

deep,

deep,

cavernous sigh.

All of a sudden, her ears perked up.

She looked to her left.

There, nestled between sheets, beneath Archie the dog, and sprawled in the shape of an "X" was Archer, her deep-sleeping brother.

But three fingers broke free from the mountain of bedding and dog. They rapped softly against the side of the bed.

Thrum-ba-bum. Thrum-ba-bum.

A song playing downstairs had coaxed Archer from his sleep. And the faint sound, like it was being carried on a breeze, was making Perri tap her toes, too.

Ba-ba-ba-bum-ta-ta-ta-ta
ta-ra-ra-babum-babum.

Perri's toes continued to TAP-TAP-TAP as she drifted off to sleep and returned to her World Series dream, happy to crowd surf from one end of fans to the other.

The next morning, something was different in Lost & Found: The Effervescent Emporium of Curiosities.

Most mornings, Aunt Bubbles had to wake the kids with a bell the size of a small car. She **bang, bang, banged** the bell with her comically large hammer until they emerged from their rooms, dragging with all the liveliness and enthusiasm of *really* old zombies.

But this morning … this morning was different. Perri and Archer happily trotted from their beds to the bathroom where they brushed their teeth. They brushed up and down, up and down. Perri combed her hair to the beat.

Comb. Comb.

Comb, Comb, Comb.

Even Archer's toenail clipping had an upbeat tempo.

The tune from last night became an anthem to their day.

They danced and TAP-TAP-TAPPED through Lost & Found. Archer, forever terrified in the Teetering Tower of Taxidermy, winked at a bear—Winked! At a bear!

Aunt Bubbles was in the kitchen. The kitchen did not have a fun name. The kids greeted her in an unusual way. "Hello, sunshine! Isn't it such a beautiful day?" Perri, who often acknowledged Aunt Bubbles with a grunt, flashed her teeth and said, "A most magnificent day!"

Aunt Bubbles prepared their usual breakfast of a slice of carrot cake and half an orange—the only way she could get them to eat vegetables and Vitamin C—and

Perri and Archer

TAP-TAP-TAPPED

on everything. They
clanged wooden spoons
on the kettle. They

shook,
shook,
shook

a tub of noodles until they danced. Archer

crunch,
crunch,
crunched

a bag of his
favorite snack.

They danced under the table and bobbed their heads to the rhythm of Aunt Bubbles's breakfast: fruit suspended in jiggly gelatin.

Even their dog Archipelago—"Archie" for short—**wagged** his tail to the beat.

Perri and Archer poured their chocolate milk to the beat of: ONE. TWO. ONE, TWO, THREE, FOUR. Aunt Bubbles even mixed her morning drink—fruits and vegetables with coconut water and just a pinch of chipotle powder to add a little pep to her wobbling step—with the rhythm of the song. Hoping that his change in mood would also mean a change in appetite, she handed Archer a glass of her healthy concoction.

Archer stopped his rhythm. "Not even today, Aunt Bubbles. *Not even today.*"

He continued **bopping.**

"Aunt Bubbles," Perri started, "can you play the song you were playing last night? I can't get it out of my head!"

"Me EITHER!" Archer agreed. "It's taking over my body! All I can think about is the Ra-ta-ta-Ra-ba-ba-babum of that song."

Aunt Bubbles chuckled. She wobbled out of the kitchen—her high-energy drink had yet to kick in—and made her way through the Haberdash-ingly Beautiful Hallway of Hats until she found the living room.

"The living room didn't have a fun name, either."

The sound filled the room. The house rocked side to side and some neighbors claimed to have even seen the house spin in the air.

Perri and Archer rushed into the living room and searched for where the magical music was coming from. Underneath the "Happy Birthday" sign that had been up since 1947 stood a strange contraption. A curious contraption, indeed.

There was a tiny box with a fancy design. It had delicate flowers and bright gemstones. There was a big crank attached to one side of the box. It looked like the tiny box was waving. On top of the tiny box was a very large horn-looking thing. It was the fanciest upside-down traffic cone Perri had ever seen. It was **HUGE,** too. Archie could surely fit in it.

"What's this?" Archer asked.

"It looks like a really, really fancy garbage can. Like that cone thing would be really good at sucking everything inside," Perri guessed.

Aunt Bubbles laughed. "This is a gramophone. Decades ago, we used it to play records. Songs were on the records."

Perri and Archer rolled their eyes. Perri whispered to Archer, "She probably used it in, like, 1555."

"On her eighteenth birthday," Archer whispered, holding back laughter.

"I heard that," Aunt Bubbles said. "And it was on my *twenty-first birthday*." She winked at the kids.

Archer and Perri walked over to the gramophone.

They turned their heads to see the name of the record and the artist.

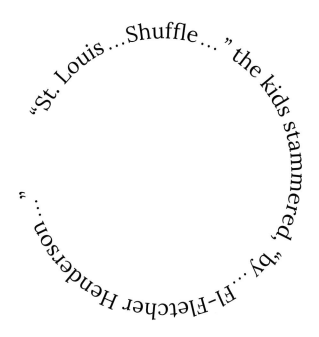

"St. Louis … Shuffle … " the kids stammered, "by … Fl-Fletcher Henderson … "

"Who is Fletcher Henderson?" Perri asked.

"Should we consult *The World Book*?" Archer offered. "But, first, let's stop at the Melodic Marina of Musical Instruments. I need to play something."

There, in the Melodic Marina,
various musical instruments
stood like egrets next to an
actual body of water.

A saxophone standing with the command and elegance of a crane caught their eye. "Perri, look! This saxophone has a 'C.H.' engraved on it. I bet those are the initials of the original owner ... but who could that be?"

"Not sure ... maybe 'Captain Hook'?" Perri suggested.

"Or 'Cheese Hog'?" Archer **giggled.** With his love of pizza, he would certainly earn the title of "Cheese Hog."

"C'mon—maybe *The World Book* will know what it means."

When they reached the rickety cart, they continued their search for Fletcher Henderson. Perri took down the "H" volume for "Henderson."

The kids read aloud: "Henderson, Fletcher (1897-1952), was a bandleader, pianist, and arranger. He was the first jazz artist to introduce the concept of the 'big band' divided into brass, reed, and rhythm sections."

BRONG

"We don't know what 'C.H.' means. And the **BRONGS** are starting. They do make a nice rhythm, though," Archer said, frantically *flipping* through *The World Book* to find a "C.H."

BRONG

Bubblets floated from the hooked and crooked grandmother clock. Perri could've sworn she saw the grandmother clock bopping to the music.

BRONG

Perri grabbed the saxophone and traced "C.H." with her dancing fingers. "I hope we find the owner. I'm sure they've missed it."

The pages of *The World Book* started to *flutter*, forcing Archer to stop his frenzied search.

"And we're off!" Perri squealed.

Perri and Archer floated through time!

Days and seconds.

Years and months.

They somersaulted

and cartwheeled past centuries and decades.

Chapter 2: AAAAAhhhhhhhhhh!

The kids landed with a **thud.**

Perri and Archer heard jazz. It flooded the streets. It **oozed** from the road. It coated the row of brownstone townhouses.

"Where are we?" Archer asked.

"*When* are we?" Perri asked.

They TAP-TAP-TAPPED their feet until they stood up and came face to face with the city. And it ... was ...

bustling.

It was as though the city itself decided to sing. The buildings rubbed up against one another, making a constant *vibration.* Growling cars zipped past, over-extending their horns as they did so. Bright, electric signs buzzed with advertisements for singers, dancers, and musicians. They lit up the already-bright sky.

Even the smells from restaurants seemed to have rhythm. They **PUFFED** from the restaurants like the burst of a horn.

WHA!
WHA!
WHA!

People crowded front stoops as others read poetry—the light in their eyes rivaling the glow of the signs. Laughter punctured the steady beat of the city.

All the while, music drifted from every open—and unopen—window.

One musical window, in particular, sparked Perri and Archer's interest. Like casting a spell, the window lured Perri and Archer in its direction.

And, as if floating on air, they glided to it. Their toes ceased TAP-TAP-TAPPING and they stretched as far as they could to peek through the window.

They rested the saxophone with the mysterious "C.H." initials on the front stoop.

With their heads resting on the ledge, they looked like pies on the windowsill. But, in this case, they were eager for music to consume them.

A woman stood inside a large, narrow room. The wallpaper reminded Perri of Lost & Found. It had a lot of **SWIRLS** and flowers. It was packed with design. Archer liked the dark wood that lassoed the room like a belt.

The woman was closing her eyes. She paused. Took a breath. And sang:

"I got the St. Louis blues, blues as I can be

That man's got a heart like a rock cast in the sea

Or else he wouldn't have gone so far from me"

"What a **beautiful** song…" Perri said, wonderstruck.

Archer—mesmerized by her smooth, silky voice—slowly nodded his head.

The woman opened her eyes and **SHRIEKED.**

"Ahhh! Who are you?!" the woman shouted.

"Uh-uh we're so sorry! Your voice is so **beautiful!**"

"We had to hear it! It pulled us here!" Archer explained.

Just as the kids were about to dart off, she called them back.

"Really? You really think it was? I have an audition later today. I'm **nervous.** I'm performing that song," the woman explained.

"It was really lovely…but a little sad," Perri said.

"Well, it is the blues, darlin," the woman said, walking over to the window.

"I'm Archer!"

"I'm Perri!"

"And my name is Honey," she said, extending her hand to greet Perri and Archer.

"Nice to meet you," Perri and Archer said in unison. They each tried to make it sound a bit musical—like Honey's beautiful singing voice.

"Is your name Honey because your voice is so sweet?" Archer asked.

She smiled.

"Is your name Honey because your smile is so sweet?" Perri asked. "Or is it because you're really fast? Do you

buzz, buzz, buzz?"

Honey laughed.

"I should keep you by my side all the time—you two are so sweet—"

"Like honey!" Perri and Archer yelled.

"Jinx, you owe me a soda," Perri said.

"My name is Honey because, when I was younger, my grandfather always said that I was the bee's knees."

"The bee's … knees?" Archer asked, perplexed. "Do bees even have knees? Wouldn't it be better to be, like, the bee's heart or something? Isn't that super important?"

"Yeah, or the bee's brain?"

"You are too funny!" Honey said. "The 'bee's knees' means excellent or terrific or wonderful."

"Ohhhh, I like that. Archer, you're the bee's knees!"

"No, Perri, you're the bee's knees!" Archer replied. "What is the opposite of the bee's knees? Like when something *isn't* so terrific? I want to say that to my dog, Archie, when he eats my maps."

Honey thought.

"Well, I'm not sure about something that's *not* so terrific. There are a lot of phrases for terrific, though."

"Like what?" Perri asked eagerly.

"Like 'Cat's meow', 'Cat's pajamas', or 'Cat's whiskers'!"

Perri and Archer **laughed** and **laughed**.

"And 'Elephant's eyebrows' and 'Gnat's whistle'!"

They roared with **laughter.**

"Wow, St. Louis really likes animal phrases," Archer said.

"What? St. Louis? We aren't in St. Louis!"

"We aren't?" Perri asked. "But you sang about St. Louis and we tap-tap-tapped to 'St. Louis Shuffle' this morning."

49

"This is Harlem—in New York City, New York!" Honey exclaimed, opening her arms w i d e to show the grandiosity of the city.

New York City!

"Is Harlem close to Legoland?" Archer asked, already thinking of his next build.

"Or-or Yankee Stadium?!" Perri asked eagerly.

"Well, I'm not sure about this ... Legoland, but we are very close to Yankee Stadium."

Archer frowned.

"I have a map of New York City from the 1850's, and I have never seen Harlem on it," Archer said.

"That's because the area we consider Harlem is quite new," Honey explained. "It has gained popularity during the Harlem Renaissance."

"The Harlem Rena-what?" Perri asked.

"The Harlem Renaissance—like ren-uh-sahnce—is the establishment of Harlem as the mecca of black cultural life."

"What does 'mecca' mean?" Archer asked.

"It means a center for a group of people," Perri explained.

"Exactly!" Honey confirmed. "Langston Hughes, Laura Wheeler Waring, and Zora Neale Hurston are important people in the Harlem Renaissance."

"What do those people do?" Perri asked.

"Well, their writings and ways of thinking challenge ideas of black life." Honey said.

"What do you mean?" Archer asked.

"Many people represent black Americans as narrow and, well, simple."

"That's not good," Perri said.

"And it's wrong," Archer added.

"That's exactly right. Writers and painters and sculptors—many people—show the **sophistication** of black American life. And the racial pride," Honey explained.

"Is the renaissance only happening here?" Archer asked, proud to use his new word.

"No. This black creativity is happening in other cities," Honey said.

"Only in the United States?" Perri asked.

"All over the world."

"Well, why is it happening now?" Perri asked.

"Many black Americans have been migrating from the South to the North. We are moving out of places in Mississippi or Georgia to cities in the Midwest and

53

on the East Coast." Honey explained.

Archer made a mental map of the migration in his head.

Honey continued, "We have moved for better jobs and better lives."

Perri and Archer stored this information deep in their brains. They wanted to remember this cultural movement—and Honey—for as long as they lived. And, if they were anything like Aunt Bubbles, they would remember until they were 400 years old.

"I know Zora Neale Hurston," Archer said. "She was—is?—a writer and anthropologist. I named my doll after her."

"My, my, she would love to know that. Well, kids, I'd better get a wiggle on."

"You're a dancer, too?!" Perri asked.

Honey laughed. "No, no. 'Get a **wiggle** on' means get going, get to it. I have an audition. I'm going to sing that song you heard me singing."

"The one about the color blue?" Archer asked.

"Not about the color blue, but about being blue— being sad. That song is a famous blues song. Bessie Smith sang it. She's my idol."

"Who is she?" Perri asked.

"She is the empress of blues. Her songs are raw and uncut—honest and genuine. Her voice and words transport me."

Perri sneaked a glance at Archer and ^raised her eyebrows at the topic of being transported.

"So, does that mean she sings about meat? Given that it's raw and uncut and all?" Archer asked.

"No, no," Honey chuckled. "She sings about everyday things—about the things that everyone experiences. Like love and loss."

"Honey, may we come to your audition?" Perri asked. "I want to hear that song one more time."

"Of course!"

As Honey changed her clothes, Perri and Archer tap-tap-tapped down the steps.

The saxophone!

"Arch, wait! We can't forget the saxophone."

"You're right. I think we would know if we forgot it—that thing is so **HEAVY,**" Archer said, massaging his arms.

Honey locked her door.

"Honey, do you know anyone with the initials 'C.H.'?" Perri asked.

"Hmmm…" Honey thought. "I don't know anyone with those initials…"

Perri and Archer frowned.

"But someone at my audition might know. Bill is most likely to be there, and he is hip to the jive."

Perri mouthed to Archer, "What does that mean?"

Archer whispered back, "I don't know. But this way of speaking is the cat's meow."

Chapter 3: The third chapter

After walking through the busy streets, Honey, Perri, and Archer arrived at Honey's rehearsal. The space was filled with people

la-la-la-la-la-la-la-ing.

"Hey, Daddy-o!"

"Hey, Mister-o...?" Archer half said, half asked.

Honey **chuckled.**

"When two cool people meet, they say 'Daddy-o,'" Honey explained.

"Perri. Archer. This is Bill. He may know who has the initials 'C.H.'"

"Pleased to meet you," Archer said.

"Hey, Daddy-o!" Perri said.

"Gimme some skin," Bill said, extending his hands to the kids.

Archer searched for a blister or scab—any piece of skin he could find. "Uh...uh, I'm sorry. I don't have any loose skin."

Bill **laughed.**

"Bill is a mighty good floorflusher. He *can dance!*" Honey said.

"Why, thank you, Honey. She's great, isn't she?" Bill said, motioning to Honey.

"She is. She's the grasshopper's ankle!" Perri exclaimed, attempting to create her own phrase.

"I'd better start warming up. Bill, you should show Perri and Archer some of your moves."

Musicians and singers swirled around Perri and Archer. There was

zooooo-ing and

oowww-ing,

ahhhh-ing and

sshhhh-ing.

While musicians warmed up their clarinets, trumpets, and drums, singers belted out the blues.

Perri and Archer loved this world. There was so much creativity and passion that they were sure the walls would give out. Everyone would be playing so hard and dancing so hard and singing so hard that the bricks would start to rattle. The mortar between the bricks would crumble away and everyone would spill out onto the street.

As they soaked in the world around them, they heard a

tip-ta-tip-ta-ra-ta-babum-babum-ra-ra-RA.

They turned around to see Bill tapping away on the floor. He was as fast as a firefly. He lit up like one, too. His smile was so bright, you could nearly see it in the reflection of his shiny, shiny shoes.

He swayed side to side and TAP-TAP-TAPPED against the wall.

After he tapped until Perri actually *did* fear the walls would give out and her fantasy would become her nightmare, he turned to the kids.

"Care to learn?" Bill inquired, raising his eyebrow.

"Yes, please!" Perri and Archer shouted.

"Swell. I'm going to teach you moves from my favorite tap dancer, John Bubbles."

"Bubbles?" said Perri and Archer in unison, followed closely by "Jinx!"

"Like Aunt Bubbles?" Archer asked, his eyes getting wider and wider by the second.

"What if—"

"Is it?"

"It can't be—well, she is, like, a kajillion years old."

"We think John Bubbles, your tap-dancing hero, might be related to our Aunt Bubbles," Perri offered.

The kids stared at Bill.

Bill stared at the kids.

He laughed. "No, no, 'Bubbles' is a nickname."

They sighed, all this time forgetting that their aunt's name was *also* a nickname.

"First, I need to see what I'm working with. Show me your best—break it down!"

Archer started doing his trusted dance move: the robot. He made his arms as stiff as a board and then, like a pendulum, swung his arms

from right to left. Lips sealed and eyes unblinking, he hinged back and back, back and forth. His movements were a bit too stiff, though—Bill thought he needed some oil.

Perri tried a more active approach. Her legs soared in the air as she hit every move with precision.

Kick!

And kick!

And kick!

And kick!

Although she didn't have the large, fluffy skirt typical of the cancan, she pretended she did by grabbing the end of her shirt.

"Alright, alright," Bill said. "That's a good start. Archer, I like your precision. Perri, I like your energy."

The kids **grinned.**

"With tap," Bill continued, "you have to focus on the rhythm. And you try to make the rhythm complex in one bar. See, like this."

Bill clicked and clacked to the songs traveling through the thick, humid air. He especially liked to hit the wooden floor with the tips of his toes. He crossed his legs over and under one another. While Perri and

Archer could hear that he was striking the ground, he moved with such speed and grace that they were sure he was hovering above the ground.

Perri and Archer began to imitate his moves. They attempted crisscrosses, hopscotches, and zigzags. But they looked like pretzels. Giant, dancing pretzels. They settled on fluttering their feet against the floor. But, instead of the melody Bill's toes made, they created a **TERRIBLE** sound.

Bill agreed.

He ended the practice session.

"Maybe we should try an instrument."

The kids stopped their—what seemed to be endless—TAPPING. It was more like noisemaking.

"I see you have a saxophone," Bill said, the sound of their TAPPING still ringing in his ears. "Do you know how to play?"

Perri and Archer shook their heads.

"We are trying to return this to someone," Perri explained. "Do *you* know how to play?"

Without saying a word, Bill lifted the mouthpiece to his lips and played a haunting melody.

"Whoa," Archer said, "you're good at everything."

Bill blushed a bit, but he didn't miss a beat. Perri and Archer were transfixed until he softly ended the sad tune.

A light bulb went off in Perri's head. "Bill, is your name a nickname? Is it different from your birth name, like Bubbles?"

Archer understood what Perri was asking—she was trying to determine if Bill's real initials were "C.H.," making *him* the owner of the saxophone.

Archer asked, "Is your name Charles Houston or Cheesy Hotdogs?" Archer *really* hoped his name wasn't "Cheese Hog." He had already decided that he would make that his nickname *the minute* they returned to Lost & Found.

Bill shook his head. "No, my birth name is Bill. I wonder who has the initials 'C.H.' Why do you ask?"

"Well," Archer began, "we found this saxophone with the 'C.H.' initials in our house, but we don't know who it belonged to."

"Yeah," Perri chimed in, "we were listening to 'St. Louis Shuffle' and wanted to go find more jazz stuff."

"The 'St. Louis Shuffle'?"

"Yep, that's the one," Perri replied.

"I think a band is performing that at the Savoy Ballroom tonight—"

"Wow, sounds **fancy.**"

"**Pos-i-lute-ly.** How those cats love to jump!" Bill replied. Perri imagined cats of all kinds leaping through the air. They would have tiny trampolines attached to their paws.

"Someone there would probably know whose saxophone it is. I'm headed there now—you interested?"

The kids nodded enthusiastically.

"But…we have to get you in. Can you

pretend to be my assistants?" Bill asked.

"Of course we can. What an adventure!"

"Hot dawg! I don't have much equipment…"
he searched for something for each kid to hold.
"Perri, you take my shoes and Archer, you take the
saxophone. We'll pretend I'm the Big Cheese with not
one *but two* assistants."

"Wow," Archer thought, "I have so many nickname
ideas: Cheese Hog! Hot Dawg! Big Cheese! What to
choose, what to choose…"

Suddenly, Archer stopped deciding.

Silky, sweet notes poured out of the room
next to them.

Bill, Perri, and Archer slowly turned to face the
music. It was as if the notes themselves reached out
and pivoted their heads.

"Honey…" Bill whispered, barely audible.

Perri and Archer nodded. Up…down…up…down. Eyes wide. Mouths open.

They were hypnotized.

She sang as if every cell in her body was singing, too.

She was powerful.

She was a force.

The spell was broken—a **thunder** of applause!

A few seconds later, Honey slammed open the door and stood in the entry, beaming.

"I take it the audition went well?" Bill asked.

Honey smiled a smile as wide as her open arms.

Bill, Perri, and Archer ran to her, cuddling in her embrace.

Perri said, "Honey, we're going to the Savoy Ballroom. Are you coming?"

"That'd be the cat's pajamas! I got the part! Maybe I'll perform at the Savoy Ballroom one day," Honey said, her eyes gleaming.

Arms crisscrossed, Bill, Honey, Perri, and Archer stepped outside to the busy street and were on their way to the swanky Savoy!

Chapter 4: Are we invited? (Of course, or else you wouldn't know what happens.)

When Perri and Archer entered the Savoy, they couldn't believe their eyes—it was a wonderland. Hundreds of people lined the walls.

Carved out in the middle of the dance floor was an area in which four or five couples showed off their skills. From their stage presence and precise moves, it was clear they were the star dancers.

They crossed their ankles over one another and swung their legs back and forth, all the while wind-milling their arms. Others **kicked** one leg high into the air and then **kicked** the other behind them—this move, in particular, reminded Perri of her kickboxing moves.

But the dancers looked much more graceful, slightly tapping their heels on the floor and kissing the sticky surface with their polished, leather shoes.

"Check out those floorflushers!" Honey shouted over the loud music. "Those rug-cutters sure can move!" As she said this, she TAPPED her feet to the music. Her movement added more ripples to the floor—a floor that was already shaking like Aunt Bubbles's breakfast.

"Hot dawg!" Archer chimed in.

"Yowza!" Bill exclaimed.

Perri and Archer swayed to the music. By dancing cheek to cheek, they imitated the other couples in the Savoy. Perri and Archer smiled their smiliest smiles and TAPPED their TAPPIEST TAPS.

"This is the best, cat's meow-ist, elephant's eyebrows-ist day ever," Perri concluded.

"Agreed," Archer said, sighing a happy sigh.

And the day improved.

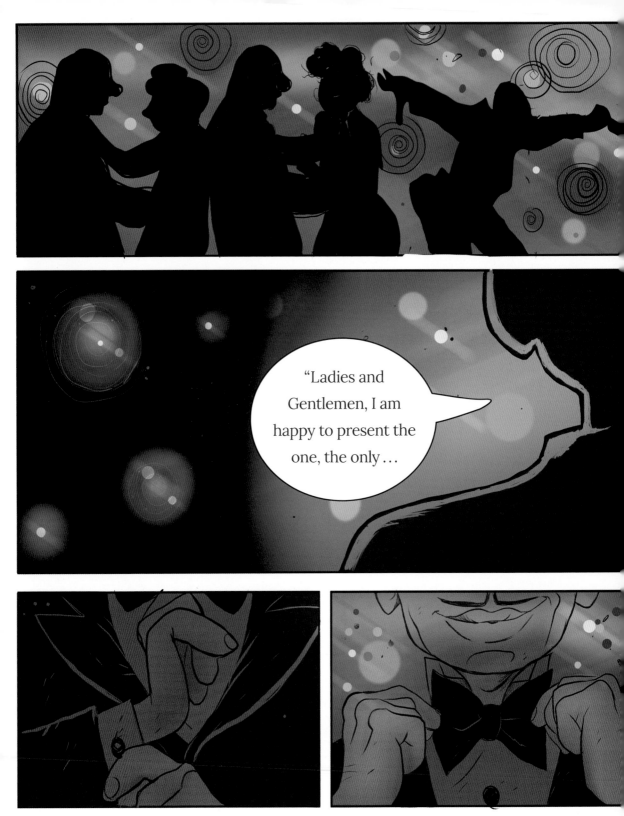

Are we invited? (Of course, or else you wouldn't know what happens.)

The noise was deafening. The hoots and hollers reminded Perri of her World Series win—even if it *was* just a dream. But this—seeing Fletcher Henderson perform—topped winning the World Series. They were watching Fletcher Henderson and his orchestra perform the *very* song that had inspired their Harlem adventure.

Bill and Honey were excited, too. Bill took Honey's hand and they were off to the center of the floor.

The saxophone was starting to weigh Archer down, so Perri carried it now. She was happy to have the prop—she pretended to play and did her best saxophonist impression. Her fingers skipped from key to key, grazing the cool metal.

Meanwhile, Archer put Bill's tap shoes on his hands and twirled and swirled around the dance floor. He clapped the tap shoes together to make a

TA-TA-TA sound.

Fletcher Henderson was more **MAGNIFICENT** than Perri and Archer could have imagined. He wore a silky, black tuxedo and had slicked-back hair. Aunt Bubbles often said people looked "sharp" and "snazzy." Before today, Perri and Archer never knew what she meant. But they sure did now.

He commanded the stage with his baton—Archer was convinced Fletcher Henderson was playing for him and Perri. He was welcoming them to Harlem.

The orchestra played in perfect unison, hitting every beat right on the mark. As they played, the men closed their eyes and wiggled their heads—**vibrating** with the music and energy.

After the Fletcher Henderson Orchestra stopped playing, the crowd collectively sighed a sigh as deep as the Grand Canyon.

But they were soon dancing again.

Bill and Honey found Perri and Archer. They were all sweaty from moving and grooving.

"Gimme some skin!" Bill yelled, reaching out to Perri and Archer.

This time, the kids knew what he meant. They

shot their sweaty hands from their sides to meet Bill's sweaty palms.

"You two were fantastic! You were the cheetah's spots!" Perri shouted.

"The hummingbird's beak!" Archer challenged.

"The snake's jaw."

"The jaguar's paw."

Perri and Archer competed with each other to propose their wackiest compliments.

Bill and Honey rolled with laughter.

"Okay, okay, this could go on for days," Bill said laughing. "You wanted to ask Fletcher Henderson about the 'C.H.' initials, right?"

Perri and Archer nodded, clutching the saxophone with their sweaty hands.

"Let's try backstage—I know a hipster who can help."

Bill, Honey, Perri, and Archer made their way backstage. Many people—fans and orchestra members—crowded Fletcher Henderson. Perri and Archer jumped up and down and waved their hands to get his attention. But Perri couldn't jump too high carrying a saxophone. Plus, how was Fletcher Henderson going to see two kids in a crowd of adults?

"Al, Al!" Bill yelled, calling to his hipster friend. "We're trying to get to Fletcher Henderson. Do you know how we can break through these people?"

Al shook his head no. "Daddy-o, there are more people around him than taxis in New York City. No *way* are you reaching him."

Bill, Honey, Perri, and Archer frowned.

"Try him," Al said, halfheartedly pointing to a man in the corner.

Perri and Archer recognized him from the performance. He mesmerized the audience—especially Perri and Archer—with his saxophone playing. But now he sat on a chair with sad eyes and a downturned smile.

Perri and Archer approached him nervously. They each tried to push the other forward. Perri succeeded—she had the help of a saxophone as a tool to prod Archer.

"Um…um…excuse me," Archer stammered. "Hello. Err—Gimme some skin." Archer quickly shot out his hand. His palms were sweatier than when they danced.

The man chuckled, taking Archer's hand. "What are two kids doing here?" the man asked. He had a twinkle in his eye.

Perri stepped forward. "We came to the Savoy to meet Mr. Fletcher Henderson."

"Well, everybody in this whole city—this whole country—wants to meet Fletcher Henderson," the man said. "What do you need him for? Maybe I could help."

"To see if he can help us return something," Archer said.

Perri presented the man with the saxophone.

Chapter 5: Stop reading this title and get a wiggle on! You're missing it!

And, oh, did he glow!

"My! Wh-wh-wh-where did you find this?" He ran his fingers up and down the keys and kissed the neck of the saxophone.

"Do you know who 'C.H.' is?" Perri asked.

"We think it stands for Captain Hook or Cheese Hog. My guess is Cheese Hog," Archer said, stifling a laugh and really hoping it wasn't, because he wanted to be called "Cheese Hog" more than anything he had ever, ever, *ever* wanted in his life.

The man chuckled. "I promise it's not Cheese Hog."

Archer breathed a sigh of relief—he really wanted that nickname.

"It stands for **Coleman Hawkins**."

"How did you know that?" Perri asked. "You were so quick."

"I'll tell you why I was so quick," the man said, leaning down to Perri and Archer. They could see the sweat on his upper lip from playing on stage. "**I** am **Coleman Hawkins**—I am 'C.H.'!"

Perri and Archer gasped.

"Oh, we found you, we found you, we found you!" Perri yelled, jumping up and down.

Coleman Hawkins, Perri, and Archer embraced.

Bill and Honey, arm in arm, watched from afar.

"How did you lose it?" Archer asked.

"Well, we were traveling from St. Louis to Chicago to perform. We stayed at a hotel one night. It was somewhere in southern Illinois," he explained. "But, we were in such a rush to jive that I forgot my axe."

"Your axc?" Perri asked.

"Why did you have an axe? Were you chopping down trees as you went?"

"Were you a jazz-playing Paul Bunyan?"

"Ha ha! I was not. 'Axe' means instrument."

"**OOOOhhhhhh,**" Perri and Archer said, nodding.

"So," Perri said, thinking aloud, "in that story about

George Washington and the cherry tree, did he cut down the tree with a violin or something? Or a saxophone?"

Coleman Hawkins **chuckled.** "I'm afraid not. 'Axe' is a term that we use when talking about jazz music. But there is more to the story."

Perri and Archer leaned in closer.

"We were almost to Chicago. We could see the skyscrapers."

Perri and Archer nodded. They had been to Chicago once—Aunt Bubbles almost fell into the river.

"I let out a cry—a cry as high-pitched as a high C. I realized I did not have my axe. But there was no way we could go back. I cried a lifetime of tears—I loved that saxophone...But now, I am reunited!" he said, his eyes lighting up.

"Mr. Hawkins," Perri asked, "could you play us

something on your axe?"

"We love 'St. Louis Shuffle'!" Archer chimed in.

And with that, Coleman Hawkins—the saxophone star of the Fletcher Henderson Orchestra—began playing "St. Louis Shuffle."

His first note was greeted with a **BRONG.**

He stopped—confused by where the **BRONG** was coming from. But he liked the competing sounds.

Bill tapped with the **BRONGS.**

It was as if Bill and the **BRONGS** were playing tag.

Every time Coleman Hawkins played a note, a **BRONG** responded.

Ta

BRONG

Sha

BRONG

Bubbles danced out of the saxophone's bell. They skipped with Coleman Hawkins's fingers as they traveled up and down the saxophone.

BRONG

Wha

BRONG

Ha

BRONGS continued complementing Coleman Hawkins's notes as Perri and Archer started traveling forward in time, forward to Lost & Found.

Chapter VI: Farewell, 1920's Harlem

The kids landed with a **thud.**

The World Book **SLAPPED** shut.

"Perri," Archer said, "I think we may still be in Harlem."

"St. Louis Shuffle" was still playing.

Perri tried extra hard to listen to the saxophone part. Now she knew that Coleman Hawkins was playing his saxophone—his axe.

"We're not in Harlem, Arch. We're back at Lost & Found."

"Then why do I still hear 'St. Louis Shuffle'?"

"Because Aunt Bubbles is still playing it."

Perri was correct.

The walls pulsed back and forth and objects jumped off the shelves and spun around. This record really was the cat's pajamas.

Perri and Archer didn't have too much energy, though. Their mouths yawned, their eyes drooped. They shuffled through the Fanciful Fortress of Forgotten Picture Frames until they reached the Expeditious Elevator of Engravings. They rode to their room, leaning on each other as they soared into the sky.

"Perri," Archer said between l o o o n g yaaawns, "can you start calling me 'Cheese Hog'?"

Perri nodded slowly. "Sure thing (yawn) Cheese Hog."

Perri and Archer tumbled into bed, flopping perpendicular to the mattress.

"Hey, Archer?"

"Yeah?"

"Tomorrow, remind me to get my initials stitched into my softball glove. I never want to lose that…" Perri said through a long yawn.

Archer murmured in agreement before they shut their eyes, yawned their last yawns and zzz-ed their first ZZZzzz's.

Their toes

TAP-TAP-TAPPING

to the "St. Louis Shuffle."

THE END

Epilogue
(that's the bit after the story)

We traveled to Harlem—not St. Louis…as we thought. Harlem is in a borough of New York City called Manhattan. It is a historic neighborhood—and not just because Perri and I visited. Starting in the early 1900's, Harlem became known as the cultural capital of black America. A mecca of black America—remember that word I learned? It's been a center of African American politics for a very long time. An organization called the National Association for the Advancement of Colored People—also known as the NAACP—set up its first local chapter in Harlem in 1911. The NAACP is a famous civil rights organization. Civil rights are the freedoms and rights that a person can have in many places: a community, a state, or a nation. You may have heard of one very famous civil rights leader—and one of *my* personal heroes—Dr. Martin Luther King, Jr.

We were in Harlem in the 1920's. That decade has been called *the golden age of jazz* or *the jazz age.* The radio had something to do with that. The "something to do with that" was that that's when commercial radio stations got started. They played live performances of the growing number of jazz musicians. More people had access to jazz—which means more people had the opportunity to *love jazz.* Harlem wasn't the only place where jazz was popular. It was also popular in New Orleans, Memphis, St. Louis, Chicago, Detroit, and Kansas City, Missouri. Hey, Arch—up for another adventure?

Our most-favorite singer, Honey, said that she liked Bessie Smith. When we returned to Lost & Found—and had a good night's sleep—we looked her up in *The World Book.* Usually, the narrator describes all the fantastical rooms through which

we travel to reach the encyclopedias. But that isn't very fun for us to describe, considering we live amongst all those rooms.

So, after traveling through the blah, blah, blah room and through the blah, blah, blah hallway, we took out the "S" volume—for Smith.

Bessie Smith lived from 1894 to 1937. She was one of the finest blues singers in the history of jazz. She was so popular and so good that she was called "the Empress of the Blues." We have a neighborhood cat named Empress, but she's black and white, not blue. I'm just kidding. The blues are a type of music. African Americans in the South started the blues. They used the music to express feelings. Fletcher Henderson played on Bessie Smith's records! She had a beautiful, powerful voice that she used to make simple songs extraordinary.

As you can see from the cover, my saxophone-playing isn't beautiful. However, it *is* powerful—it even cracked

notes! Maybe I'm better at singing.

Another person in the illustration of the Harlem Renaissance on page 53 was Langston Hughes. He was an African American author known for his poetry. He was born in either 1901 or 1902. He died in 1967. The rhythm of jazz and blues music influenced the rhythm of his poetry.

With his poetry, he explored race pride and black culture. And you know how I explore things with maps? Or how Perri and I explore other cultures when we return objects? Langston Hughes's exploration wasn't really like that. Perri and I explore cultures and peoples *different* from our own. But Langston Hughes explored black life in America *as a black person in America.*

Now it's both of us. Remember how we told you to pay attention to the orange words? Well, now we are going to tell you why. It's because those words are difficult words that either we learned or we used or the writer of this book put in to make the book better. Also, some of these words have multiple meanings. So we defined them in terms of how they are used in this book.

cancan: a Parisian dance that involves a lot of kicking

cavernous: huge; immense

ceased: stopped; finished; came to an end; what our adventure did when we returned the saxophone

coaxed: persuaded; like how Aunt Bubbles coaxes us to take our vitamins

commanded: dominated; ruled; like what Perri doesn't do when she plays the saxophone . . . or sings

contraption: machine; device

effervescent: high-spirited; joyous; bubbly; Aunt Bubbles

grandiosity: when something is impressive

idol: a person's favorite person; Aunt Bubbles to me and Archer

lured: drawn in; tempted

mesmerized: when someone is so, so, so enchanted by something or someone

perpendicular: at a 90-degree angle to something

rapped: knocked; not in the sense of what Aunt Bubbles does when she listens to hip hop music

sophistication: elegant

stumper: a puzzling question or problem

swanky: fancy; Fletcher Henderson

transfixed: astonished; like mesmerized

triumphant: victorious; feeling you have when you've won something

unison: together; at the same time

wafting: traveling through the air; what the smell coming from a fresh pie does

Cat's meow, cat's pajamas, cat's whiskers: Great!

Get a wiggle on: Get going.

Daddy-o: greeting between two cool people

Hip to the jive: Cool

Hot dawg: Great!; on Archer's list of nicknames

Bee's knees:
Terrific!

Gnat's whistle:
Terrific!

Floorflusher:
super-good dancer

Elephant's eyebrows:
Terrific!

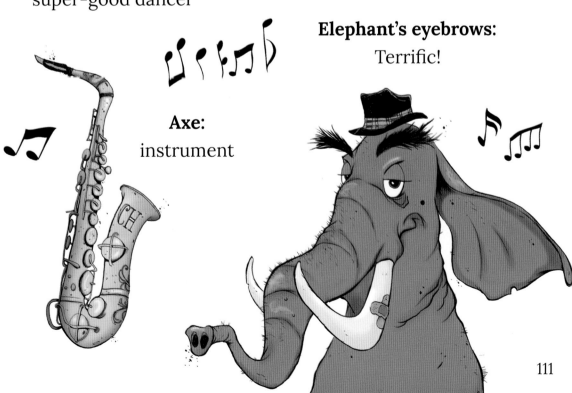

Axe:
instrument

Written by
Madeline King

Illustrated by
Scott Brown

Directed by Tom Evans
Designed by Melanie Bender
Illustration colored by Francis Paola Lea
Cover and additional illustration by Dave Shepherd
Proofread by Nathalie Strassheim

With special thanks to:

Robbin Brosterman and Lucie Luddington of The Bright Agency,
Evie Beckett, Anne Fritzinger, Grace Guibert, Linda King, Mohan Kulik,
the Perry family, Rubric Sane, Rebecca Sullivan, and Lillian Tanner.
Oh, and Aunt Bubbles.

World Book, Inc.
180 North LaSalle Street, Suite 900
Chicago, Illinois 60601
USA

For information about other "Lost & Found" titles, as well as other World Book
print and digital publications, please go to www.worldbook.com.

For information about other World Book publications, call 1-800-WORLDBK (967-5325).

For information about sales to schools and libraries,
call 1-800-975-3250 (United States) or 1-800-837-5365 (Canada).

Library of Congress Cataloging-in-Publication Data for this volume has been applied for.

Lost & Found
ISBN: 978-0-7166-2807-1 (set, hc.)

Saxophone Stumper
Perri and Archer's adventure during the Jazz Age
ISBN: 978-0-7166-2810-1 (hc.)

Also available as:
ISBN: 978-0-7166-2816-3 (e-book)

Printed in China by RR Donnelley, Guangdong Province
1st printing July 2019